Black Rose-
The Final Thirteen
THE ULTIMATE TWIST

KEISHA SEALS
IN COLLABORATION WITH
LAKEISHA DOYLE AND DESAREE SEALS

authorHOUSE®

AuthorHouse™
1663 Liberty Drive
Bloomington, IN 47403
www.authorhouse.com
Phone: 1-800-839-8640

Published by AuthorHouse 2/10/2014

ISBN: 978-1-4918-5821-9 (sc)
ISBN: 978-1-4918-5819-6 (hc)
ISBN: 978-1-4918-5820-2 (e)

Library of Congress Control Number: 2014901532

*Cover designed by Mr. Chris "CK" Moore of Charakter Entertainment,
email: charakta@gmail.com*

Contents

DEDICATED TO:

Shirley Doyle, Lenora Doyle, Keshawn Seals and Suzette Phillips; Mrs. Barbra Johnson (Lakeisha's adopted foster mother) for inspiring her to be a writer by ripping up her poem and telling her, she would never amount to anything; she realized her true passion within herself. To my brother in law, Prentice J. Thames-Jackson, R.I.P., gone but never forgotten thank you for your encouragement. Thank you for the memories. This is dedicated also to all the females who dream their dreams, this book shows that dreams really do come true.

Acknowledgements

I would like to thank my sons' Daquan Doyle, Shawn Seals II and George T. Jackson Jr. their inspiration and their feedback. To my mother, Helen Jones, my daughter LaTeashea Jackson-McNair and my mother in law Catherine V. Jackson, for their love and support. Special thanks to my daughter Desaree Seals and my niece Lakeisha Doyle Johnson for their encouragement and their correspondences materials incorporate throughout this book. Last but certainly not least my wonderful husband George T. Jackson Sr. for his unfounded belief in my dreams and my friend, Adrienne Morris for putting up with my husband and me. We could not have done this without you.

Chapter One

IT WAS A cold winter night, the roads, cars and roof tops were covered with fresh white falling snow; it was such a beautiful view. All of the houses were decorated on the block with beautiful blinking Christmas lights glistening off the snow onto both of the sidewalk and the streets. The smoke coming from the chimney of the houses, the foggy windows gave me the impression that the fireplaces were lit up to keep their homes warm from the cold outside. The sweet smelling aroma of hot chocolate in the air made it feel more and more like Christmas, making me think of my Grandmother. She would make me her famous hot chocolate with marshmallows which always gave me a feeling of peace, joy and warmth. People were walking down the street holding hands; laughing, singing and dancing in the snow, yelling Merry Christmas to the neighbors as they walk pass the house. Twelve Christmas carolers singing Christmas songs fill the night with soft beautiful music. They were all bundled up in their big winter coats and their heavy snow boots, keeping their feet warm from the cold; their hands were frozen and their lips were shivering from the cold. Christmas was always my favorite holiday even when I was a child I could not wait until Christmas. My brother and I would help my mother decorate the Christmas tree and bake chocolate chip cookies for Santa Claus. As the snow continued to fall covering the houses and the streets, I heard the sound of kids playing outside my window, they were making snow men and having snow ball fights reminded me of my early childhood when I use to play outside with my brother having snowball fights. At one point I wanted to jump out the window and make a snow angel but I couldn't, it would have just remind me of the time when my older brother buried me in the snow when I was younger causing me to shiver down my spine. As I look out the window I feel a warm hug push against my back and a soft warm whisper in my ear, "saying isn't it beautiful" As she began holding me tight, "I could feel the love." She said, "James, *"The Grinch That Stole Christmas* is coming on Television in an hour, would you like to watch it with me?" First I need to walk to the store to get some eggnog and snacks for us to eat when we watch the movie. I followed Rose into the living room where the light on the television sparkle at her face making her twice as beautiful. I never thought I could ever love anyone as much as I loved Rose, from the top of her head to the bottom of her feet. Rose is truly a beautiful woman. She was 5'9 with long beautiful dark brown hair; tanned complexion with a truly amazing figure, she is half Indian and half black but could pass for a Hispanic female. She weighed about 125 pounds, slender with curve, a butt the size of an onion, beautiful enough to make you cry. Her breast was the size of a pineapple, beautiful round and perfect with no sag or fat, not too big, not to small. She had a tattoo on her lower back, a picture of a rose instead of her putting her name, which I thought was cleaver. She had a belly piercing heart ring and diamond earrings that hung to her shoulder I truly admired Rose incredible body. She has the most beautiful long slender legs, like a model figure. She was extremely educated, strong personality and very independent. As I opened the door for us to head out to the store, I was hit by multiples snow balls thrown by kids laughing and running off. I heard a giggle coming from off the side of me. It was coming from Rose trying so hard not to laugh as I clean the snow off my face, "Oh you think that's funny Rose?, let's see how funny it is when I hit you with this snowball." We played in the snow for almost an hour then we headed to the store. On our way back, Rose was shivering and shaking from the cold. Her nipple was poked out her cheeks was apple red, her lips were shivering and slightly parted from being cold. Once we returned back to the house I helped Rose out of her coat and brought her a blanket, so she could lie on the couch to get warm until I could bring her a cup of hot chocolate. I brought the snacks in the living room so we could eat them while we watch the movie. As I lay on the couch with Rose in the opposite direction from her, I was able to admire every part of her body and I wouldn't trade her for anything. My thoughts were interrupted when I heard Rose soft voice. "James, why are you not watching the movie? It is starting now." I'm sorry about that, I was just thinking about the first time we met and how I knew it was love at first sight, she blushed, I could see her cheeks getting pink, at that one point the television was now watching us. I remember that day like it was yesterday, my ex-girlfriend and I broke up and I needed time to think, to make a long story short, I treated myself to a nice lunch at the restaurant in the city. I was so mesmerized by her beauty when she came into the restaurant to grab her coat which was behind the chair I was sitting in. "Can I help you? You like what you see?" said Rose grabbing her coat. Why yes, you can help me I was looking at my menu and I realize you were not on it. By the way my name is James. "Well James sorry to have disappointed you. You are welcome to put in a complaint to the owner of this restaurant, which would be my dad, if you think the menu mislead you" Rose said with a smile on her face. It's nice, I told you my name and I think it will be only fair if you tell me yours, she responds by saying, "they call me Rose." I smiled and said it's nice to meet you, well Rose do you have a phone number that I could call you and ask you out to dinner next weekend? Rose giggled and said, it really depends on if you have a wife and kids at home. James laughed and said, "no Rose, no wife or kids to my knowledge unless you heard otherwise." We exchange phone numbers and I let her go her way, later that night I had got a phone call from a strange number. At first I thought it was my ex- girlfriend Jenna, so I did not bother to answer. The phone started to ring continuously again and again; finally, I could no longer ignore it so I answered the phone in a deep loud voice "HELLO!" Then I heard this soft sweet voice "Hi, James this is Rose, did I catch you at a bad time? Sound like you are upset." I was shocked I did not think she was going to call me. I answer and said "no, this is a perfect time, how are you doing?" Since that night we talked and talked, and then we became friends before we became lovers as the days and months went by. I still can't believe that we have been together for five years now. I can always tell when Rose get upset, any time the subject of her ex- husband comes up as if he was abusing her and she was trying to forget all about how cruel the beating were. When I ask her about how her husband died, she would give me the same answer each time, "natural causes" but I could tell that was not the truth. I did not want to get to personal so I left it alone and I hope maybe one day she would be comfortable enough to trust me with the truth. She gave me a look, and then she began to kiss me with her nice soft sweet lips. I love to have gone further but it was three o'clock in the morning. I have to get up by five for my business trip which gives me three hours to sleep. Rose was my first true love and next year I plan on making her my wife.

Chapter Two
A Year Later....

LOOKING FOR MY keys with roses in my hand; I was so happy to be back home, I didn't even realize that the keys was in my hand, I was so happy that nobody was around to see how stupid I look looking for a key that was in my hand. I quickly went inside hoping I could smell that sweet sensational dinner on the stove, Roses famous welcome back home steak dinner along with candle lit making it a romantic evening for us. In fact, the house was completely the opposite, a complete mess, cold, dark, and dishes look as if they had been there for weeks. The house was so quiet and dusty as if it had been abandoned for years. I thought for a moment maybe I came into the wrong house or Rose moved out. I was hoping to find a note, telling me that she went to the grocery store or out with her friends. When I call her cell phone I only got her voicemail which in fact it was not like Rose. That's when I began to worry, then I remember that Rose told me a couple of weeks ago over the phone that she was diagnose with cancer so I had to be mindful that she would not be the same as before and in fact she may have been upstairs sleeping so I scream her name. "Rose I'm home, are you here?" I didn't get an answer but the closer I got to the bedroom I heard loud groaning as if someone was in tremendous pain. So I ran up the stairs, open the bedroom door, Rose looks lifeless as if she been in the bed for months sick. She was skinny as a toothpick and all of her long brown gorgeous hair was gone. Her skin tone was very pale as if all the color had ran out of her face, this was not the Rose I remember she did not look like herself in fact she looks like a stranger to me. The Rose I remember was completely beautiful, I rush to the bedside with tears in my eyes; I said, "Rose, I'm calling the hospital now, this can't be cancer. Rose, where is your Medicine? Rose seemed to be having a hard time answering me. She was so weak, cold and brittle. I laid in the bed next to her, holding her close to my chest to keep her warm, tears running down my face. Rose looked up at me and said, "James, please don't cry I'm ok sweetie, just tired. I'm happy your home, I am so sorry I didn't mean to do this to you, I love you with all my heart and soul." She was so delicate and scrawny I felt as if I was hugging myself. I responded to her by saying "You have no reason to be sorry because you are sick, I love you Rose and I want you to marry me and become my wife." I heard the ambulance siren outside then the banging on the door; I look down at Rose and said, "hold on love help is here" She smile and within minutes I heard her breathing become shallow, body stiffen and right at that moment I knew Rose had died in my arms; they work on her for nearly an hour to bring her back to life, but there was nothing they could do to bring her back. She was pronounced dead at the house. It felt as if I cried a life time that night; I lay in the bed for about a week after Rose died trying to get some understanding why she died. I did not want to get out of bed this particular day because this is the day I have to say good bye to the love of my life, my best friend. I do not know how I am going to get pass this day. I still cannot believe Rose is dead this feels like a bad dream that I'm trying to wake up from. I fear every minute of it, it's been raining all day and I am getting dress to go to Rose's Funeral. I have not slept in a week missing her, waking up hoping all this was a nightmare and Rose is still alive. I arrived at the church it is full with people all dressed up crying. Rose coffin sat in front of the church open for all her friends and families to view her body. I walk very slowly to the coffin, when I got up close to her I wanted to hold her, tell her to wake up and everything will be okay.

The tears ran down my face because I still can't believe that I will never be able to see her walk through the door, hear her voice, or hold her inside of my arms. Within minutes my eyes was red and puffy from crying then out of nowhere I smelled this sweet fragrance behind me the same White Diamond perfume that Rose use to wear; when I turned around it was Rose's mother Jackie, she gave me a big warm hug. Rose looks so much like her mother as if they could have been twins; tall, slim and beautiful. "Hello James, How are you holding up? I want to thank you for being there for her, she loved you so much" Jackie said, trying to console me; I answer her, "I'm holding up the best way I can, I wish Rose was still here. I am so mad that the Doctor did not catch this cancer at an early stage, maybe she would have been alive now instead of in that damn coffin, and she does not deserve to be there." Rose's mother had this puzzled look on her face, like this was news to her. Then finally she said "James I am sorry Rose did not die of cancer, she died of AIDS. She has been living with it for 10 years she got it from her husband that's how he died, Rose did not tell you?" I felt my blood getting hot, my heart going cold and rage over my body. I respond in a loud yelling voice AIDS, "Rose had AIDS that's not what she told me. She told me that she had cancer for five years and we been together for the whole five years having unprotected sex." He stormed over to Rose coffin pushing it over forcing her body to fall on the floor out of the coffin, next he stood over her body yelling "I hope you rot in hell for this." He left with a crowd of people watching in shock and horror while the pallbearers tried to place Rose body back into her coffin. The pastor tried his hardest to maintain the crowd by calming them down so he could gain control over the situation for what just had happened, so that the funeral could go on for Rose's families and love ones can have a peaceful farewell service. Be comfortable in their time of grief and be able to share any of their reflection of Rose life; to honor her name but after what just happened the mood was damper, some was full of rage, others were mentally destroyed by this monstrous act of evil on the day her family grieve their loss. Then there were others who were frozen in shock and were left completely speechless because never in their life have they witness anything like this as if they were in a horror movie or a bad dream and just can't seem to wake up. When he returned back to the apartment he packed up anything that belong to Rose and any memories of Rose, he left it in the apartment with a dozen of black roses spread all over the bed with a picture of Rose in the center.

Chapter Three

THAT NEXT MORNING James woke up feeling guilty about pushing over Rose coffin, so he decided to go to her burial site to apologize to her. When he arrived to the grave yard, James begin to have second thoughts as to why he was there and how could the only woman he loved left him with such an open wound. James continued walking until he saw Rose tombstone. James eyes started to fill up with water as his hands grazed against her name. He broke down in tears while resting his head and arms against the tombstone hoping Rose could hear him but unfortunately he did not get any reply. James lifts up his head and began talking. At this moment I don't know where to start. Why! Why me? Rose, what have I done? I gave you love out of this world, yet you punish me and now that you're dead I can't get an answer out of you. When James was talking, his eyes was wandering around the grave yard when he notice on the right of the tombstone label was David Parker

Jr., the son of Rose Parker. James blinked twice hoping that the tears that flooding his eyes, making it very blurry that he was just seeing things and the tombstone was not really Rose son, so he wipes his eyes until it was completely dry then he looked again and it was in fact the tombstone of her son. All he could think about is how cans this woman who claimed to love him keeps a secret of her having a son from him while lying about her life. Within minutes James went from feeling guilty to rage, his blood began to boil and once again that same rage that surface at the funeral return back making him angry. James seems to be a bit puzzled when he saw another person name written on the plaque right next to Rose name; he kicked the tombstone a few times then spit on her son's gravel all the while shouting." Rot in hell you will pay for this like every other woman will pay for my pain". James was so upset because Rose whole life was a lie, the Rose he thought he knew, he did not know, maybe her name wasn't even Rose. Two months went by since Rose funeral and his visit to the cemetery. He woke up by the sound of the Catholic Church bell ringing at 7:00 am on a Sunday morning. This particular morning the bell sounded extremely louder, like if I was sleeping in front of the church but I wasn't. I could never hear the church bell but on this particular day it woke me out of my sleep like a bad hangover. Last night was the first night in a long time I had been feeling a lot better since the funeral. However, when I went out with some co-workers and had a few drinks, it felt so strange being out. It's really been a long time since I had a drink damn it felt so good. I still can't believe how long it's been since Rose died and I have not been to church since the day I went to Rose funeral. I remember every Sunday Rose and I would get up and get dress for church, Rose loved going to church and so did I. But after Rose died my love to go to church all changed. I never would think in a million years that I would despise going to church when majority of my childhood was being in church with my parents. I have been so angry with God since Rose died, I thought that God had brought Rose into my life then took it all away leaving nothing for me to love and to be loved. What have I done to make God so mad at me? That he punished me to be alone, I guess when God blesses you; you are not supposed to be selfish and forget about him. Yesterday morning, I finally got back some of my strength to go see the doctor because I had been sick since Rose died and now I am waiting for my results. Last night was so amazing I forgot what it was like to be single again, so many beautiful women approached me to dance, bought me drinks and even handed me their numbers. As I sat here day dreaming about last night, I was startled when the phone rang,

"Hello . . . Y . . . e . . . s, this is James" I dropped the phone in total shock when the doctor gave me my result, I could not believe that I was HIV positive I began to feel a pain in my chest as I drop to the floor on my knees. I asked the doctor again was he sure that the result was right could it have been in error? I was in total shock and refused to believe what the doctor said was true. I was so mad that I started yelling at the doctor saying that his lab made an error and I want them to redo the test but the doctor kept saying I'm sorry Mr. Sinclair, I wish I did not have to tell you this news, but if you need to come in and talk to me or my social worker we are here to help, again I am so sorry but if you come in next week Wednesday we could start you on pills and treatment to help you. I agree to come in and get help but after the doctor hung up the room felt like it was spinning out of control, I dropped down on the floor in total denial and then I started crying so uncontrollable that the pain got more and more stronger that I felt like I could not breathe and all the air left the room. Somehow I fell asleep and when I woke up I remember the phone call that I had got from the doctor and could not believe Rose gave me HIV and did not tell me she had it. What had I done to her to make her do such a thing like this? I thought she loved me and would never do anything to hurt me or jeopardize my future plans. She had me believing she wanted a future with me and so much more, if I could I would dig that bitch out of the grave and beat the living hell out of her. I am so mad that if I can't have a full life then I will be damn if anybody else will have a full life. As long as I live on this earth it will be all about me. Love and women are no longer in my dictionary. Love and women can't be, trust me. This is a huge world and tomorrow is not promised to anyone especially me; if I die I know I won't be dying alone. From this day on revenge is a bitch. No more sobbing and thinking about Rose, she's in a place where I know for sure her soul will pay for what she did and I truly believe the hell she's giving me is the hell she's living in. My mother always taught me to have respect for all females but today, I no longer have respect for any female and you can all thank Rose for that. I will enjoy the rest of my life even if it kills me. I was never the scandalous type or bad boy but the pain inside of me started to create a negative thought in my mind. After all that thinking I became hungry, so I made me a sandwich and drunk a beer. I reach for the phone to call my mother to talk but when I started dialing I heard a woman on the other end yell hello. I know that I was not done dialing my mother's phone number so who was this woman on the other side of my receiver. She may have accidently dial my phone number first. The woman on the other line was asking to speak to some guy name Jason. For a moment her voice sound just like Rose and it gave me goose bumps, it was so soft and sweet like as if she was innocent. My next step was to get her mind off the person she was calling, and put all her attention on me. So I said, "I am sorry your boyfriend gave you the wrong number" the woman began to laugh, "No I was not calling my boyfriend, I was calling my brother," I asked her would she like for me to take down a message for him." The woman started laughing so hard finally she said, "No thank you, you do not know my brother." I asked her what her name was and she said her name was Brenda. I asked her if she had any plans for tonight and I would really like for her to be my date tonight. I explained to her that today was my birthday and all my closest friends and family already made other arrangements that they could not help me celebrate my birthday and I did not want to be eating dinner alone tonight. She believed the lie about today being my birthday and agreed to have dinner with me. I clean up the house, change my bed sheets set out two glasses and a bottle of wine in a bucket just in case she comes back to my place I will be ready for her. I got dress look in the mirror and for the first time I saw myself since Rose died. I am 6'3, weight 162 lbs, milk chocolate complexion, and dark green eyes, with a 6 pack stomach and long dark brown micro dreads, damn I'm a handsome man then I grabbed my jacket headed to the door and said let the games begin, this one is for you Rose. On my way to the restaurant I stop by the flower shop and purchased a black rose and told them to engrave the number one on the rose, the florist looked puzzled when he hand her one black rose with a request for her to engrave a one on it. I explained by saying the number 1 on the rose is because she is my number one. The florist laughs because she thought that James was trying to be funny with one black rose, she thought James made an honest mistake by picking up a black rose that in fact he probably meant to pick up a different color after she heard his explanation. I saw nothing funny about what I asked for, "If you can't help me find someone else who will?" The florist apologizes and said her intention was not to be rude, but each rose has its own symbolic meaning. The florist explained to James that black rose means death, hate and revenge; red rose means love; yellow rose means friendship or new beginning; lavender rose means love at first sight; blue rose means mystery or attaining the impossible; and red and white rose together means unity. Sir, now that I explain to you the different roses and there meanings would you prefers another color instead of black. I can't believe that she went through all this about some roses, like it was my first day on the job. Then this woman had the nerve to ask me if I wanted another color after twenty minutes of explaining the meaning of each rose, without realizing what I was thinking in my head came out of my mouth "Hell No! Give me the black rose with the number 1 on it, and next time you want to give your opinion when nobody asks you just mind your business and do your job." I left the flower shop a little irritated and in a hurry to get to the restaurant for my date. When I arrived at the restaurant Brenda was already seated at the table. As I approach the table she rises to introduce herself. She was not my average type of woman in fact she was a short, dark skin and a little on the heavy side. Brenda is wearing black leather tight spandex, red low cleavage blouse with red and white stiletto shoes, she looks sensational in that outfit; she was very classy looking. Although, she was nothing like Rose; she still was a pretty woman. Brenda was very fascinated that I brought her a black rose instead of red, she really like the rose and never paid attention to the number on it, I really enjoyed my conversations with Brenda; she has such a great personality, smart and funny. After dinner, I invite Brenda back to my house for a night cap and a movie, I was surprised that she agreed to come back to my place; when we get to the house I help her take her coat off and escort her to the living room. She requests to use the bathroom

I told her to the left inside is the master bedroom. When Brenda returns from the bathroom she had sarcastic smirk on her face. "Do you normally set your bed with red satin sheets and black rose petals all over the bed, and a bucket of wine on ice with two wine glasses next to each other? I laugh and giggle. "Do you normally snoop around a person bedroom when asked to go to the bathroom? I hope I don't have to search your pockets." We both laughed and sat down on the couch. It's getting kind of late and I have to get up in the morning. I really enjoyed being in Brenda's company, so I plead for her to stay, at least to have a drink of wine with me to toast to my birthday she agrees to stay just an hour. I dim the light and played some music and grab a couple bottles of wine, after about twenty minutes of drinking wine I ask her to slow dance with me. By the way she was stumbling to keep from falling and her words were no longer understandable, I can tell Brenda was on the intoxicated side; she became very flirtatious and started saying "how attractive I was and that she wanted to make love to me." I was shocked by her words then I asked her was she sure that she wanted to stay the night with me. I knew that she was too intoxicated to understand what she was asking me to do to her. Brenda starting kissing my ears, neck and then out of nowhere I felt her tongue on my chest licking and kissing all over me, as I felt her unzip my pants as if she wants to see Mt. Rush More. I grab her hand and said, "Are you sure you want to do this?" Her hands already gracing my manhood; I felt my manhood rise as she stroked it up and down. "Brenda", I said you don't have to do this, by this time I couldn't finish my sentence because Brenda's mouth was already thrust over my manhood bobbing her head up and down like she was a pro. I let out a cry that I had never knew I had inside of me and my eyes started rolling behind my head as if I was having a seizure as Brenda kept going deeper and deeper. Oh my God, I could not believe how deep throat Brenda was, as if she was swallowing my manhood whole and I could see it in her throat, it was so good that I lost my balance and fell over. I started to remove Brenda spandex and her g-string and I begin to rub my finger across her clit and then I slide it inside of her, first one finger until I was able to put my whole hand in her Vagina. She was so wet and juicy that I put my hot warm lips on her vagina blowing hot air then I stuck my tongue inside her vagina licking and sucking slow and soft. She began murmuring softly to me and let out a cry of pleasure then I picked Brenda up and carry her into the master bedroom and lay her on the red satin sheet cover with black rose petals. I look down at her face and noticed how truly beautiful, Brenda was. She pulled me on top of her as I slid my manhood inside of her. She started to moan grabbing my long dark brown dreads hair like as if my big manhood were hurting her. I started sucking on her breast trying to take away some of the pain from my big manhood as I thrust deeper and deeper and harder and harder, I could feel my sperm building up then I explode all inside Brenda and we both pass out from exhaustion. That morning when I woke up Brenda was still lying next to me with nothing on, I remember making love to her a couple of times during the night. Brenda had a smile on her face like she was totally satisfied then I noticed that we did not use condoms at all. I got this sick feeling in my stomach, I realized that it was not my fault it was Rose who gave it to me first, so blame it on Rose? Then, I heard this soft voice "good morning James, I hope you enjoyed your birthday last night, I really enjoyed myself." I responded, "Yes I did and thank you." Brenda explained that she was sorry that she could not stay any longer because she has to go and meet a business partner for lunch to discussed business and she will call me later. I was so happy that she had to go. I got up and dropped her off, back at the restaurant to get her car so she could go home and shower before her business lunch. When I returned home I took a shower and got dress. I remember all those other female phone numbers that I received the other night when I went out drinking with my co-workers, came across a number of a woman by the named Jackie. So I figure what the hell I'll call her; to my surprised she answered the phone. I explained to her that today was my birthday and I was wondering if she would like to have dinner with me so I would not have to spend it alone. She agreed to have dinner with me tonight. I took a quick nap to rest up for my dinner date tonight. I woke up so I could clean up the house, change the bed sheets and set out two glasses on the table and put a bottle of wine in a bucket full of ice for a night cap. On the way to the restaurant I stop by the flower shop and brought another black rose with the number 2 engraved on it, this time the clerk said nothing and let me go on my way. When I arrived at the restaurant Jackie had not arrived yet, so I waited at the bar for her, she finally arrived 15 minutes late. Jackie was incredibly beautiful; she has long golden legs and long jet black hair and she had a light brown skin. When she walked you could see every beautiful curve, she had a hell of a body any man would be happy to stand next to her. She apologized for being late, I smiled and said it was okay; dinner and conversation was exceptional. I invited her back to my place, first she refused because she had to get up early, but I persuaded her into just coming over for a few minutes. After a couple of rounds of love making, Jackie and I had fallen asleep. I woke up to the alarm on my phone going off time for me to wake Jackie. She looked beautiful with the black and red satin sheet covering her beautiful body and hair scatter all over the bed, looking like an angel. I watched her in amazement for a moment before I woke her up. I could not believe how beautiful she was as I watch her get dress. She is beautiful with or without clothes on. I drop Jackie at the restaurant so she could get her car. Once I returned home I took a shower and went back to bed, I noticed my answering machine light was blinking two miss calls. I guess I will check it when I wake up.

Chapter Four

LATER THAT EVENING, I jump up because I could not believe I slept this late; it was almost 3pm, late in the afternoon. I been out every night with a different female starting with Monday night was Brooklyn she received the 3rd rose, Brooklyn was very special to me because she was a transsexual, a man living his life as a female; it was my first time being with a man. One would say I'm gay that's their opinion because I don't see anything wrong with being with a man? I can remember being with Brooklyn as if it happen yesterday how she walked oops I mean how he walked with grace and confidence as a woman but with big broad shoulders, muscular legs, the tightest round ass prefect as an onion that forces you to cry and a hand as big as a basketball player to wrap around my penis with the intention to stroke at the same time, as he place it inside of his mouth as if he were swallowing my penis whole. The deep throat on him was making me think that my penis is touching his stomach making an explosion inside of his mouth, ejaculating in full force enough to make a grown man scream of pleasure he never felt before. Body shaking, heart racing and when I think it's over Brooklyn just got started, he would get on top of me, place my penis inside of his tight ass and rode me up and down, in circular motion then he back his ass all the way on my penis making me feel like my penis is touching his spine. I got more pleasure out of fucking Brooklyn then I did fucking a woman; believe me when I say, he sure knows how to please his man. One night of pleasure for me but a whole life of sickness for him, do you think I feel guilty for not telling him that I am positive, laughing to himself as he said out loud, "Hell No", Rose it's all fair in love and war; it's just that I'm going to finish it. This all started because I loved a woman who hid behind a mask of unclaimed sickness with lies, deceit, and betrayal when she knew it was her fault. Now I walk this road a dead man. I die, we die, and I refuse to die alone and I'm taking everybody with me so when you think I love you, you better think again. Then Tuesday night was Diamond 4th rose, Wednesday night was Jayda 5th rose; Thursday night was Sophie 6th rose, and Friday night was Emily 7th rose. Damn, I still can't believe how easy it was to have sex with seven females since Rose died; I handed out seven

Black roses with numbers on it to keep track of how many females I had sex with. The more I lay in the bed the later it got with me reminiscing about the seven females I slept with night after night and transmitted the virus. I don't feel sorry for these females because they chose to sleep with me unprotected and without even knowing me, even the smart females have one stupid moment. These females desire to be infected, damn dumb ass girls sleeping with a man unprotected they don't even know. Wow, I look at the clock it was 5:30pm, the day was almost gone. I dressed quickly, put on a pair of loose—fitted blue jeans, white sneakers, and pullover white sweater along with a blue sport jacket. I noticed that the answering machine was still blinking as if it was full of messages, but I was in no mood to check the answering machine so I left it blinking. I grabbed my keys made a dash for the door, caught glimpse of myself in the mirror and noticed the dark twisted soul in my eyes looking back at me so eager to find my next victim. I wonder if I go to the grocery store how many single females will I be able to convince to go out with me and come back to my place for a night cap. I stepped out into the hallway, locked the door and rush down the stairs before it got any later. I did not want the night to come and I am home alone. I have been haunted by Rose death every night since she died. It's like a continuous nightmare of Rose memory in my head and the constant dream night after night of Rose lying in the coffin full of AIDS and what I had to look forward to dying of. Tonight is supposed to be a full moon and I am not going to spend tonight alone. Just then my cell phone rang. It was a female that I met a few weeks ago on a plane to Chicago when I was on my business trip and I told her if she ever came to New York to give me a call. I was surprised that she remembered my number. She said she called to see if I had plans tonight because her flight back to Chicago is a delay until the next day. Damn, this is what you call pure luck that she would call me since the time I gave her my number three month ago. I could not believe she kept my phone number this long and called. I was in total shock. Isabella is as beautiful as her name and very intelligent; she is a business consultant like me, traveling and closing business deals. I picked her up from the Airport and went out to eat and that the night she stayed at my place instead of in a cold lonely dark hotel. I promised her breakfast in bed and a ride back to the Airport, we stayed up half the night laughing and talking. Isabella took a long shower which she asked me to join her, I was more than happy to join her. The soap and water glisten off her body, sending my body into over drive. I could not control my excitement and the belly of the beast had been awakened. We made love in the shower and then we made love again in my bed, it felt like Paradise; I felt like I died and went to heaven. I never felt this alive in my life. I wanted more and more of Isabella, I felt like I could not get enough of her. She was like a drug that I was craving for. What have this woman done to me to make me react this way. I never one time thought about Rose. Then the alarm clock went off and the spell was broken. I got up and took Isabella back to the Airport, I handed her the 8th black rose and told her thanks for the night. Isabella was the first female that I really hated to have given her the black rose, but I had to stay focus on passing the virus and remember not to fall in love no matter who it is. As I stroll through my cell phone contact list, trying to find this phone number of this woman that I met at a grand opening of an Art gallery show. Her name was Alexis, that woman had a body of a goddess and the face of an angel, she is so soft spoken and intellectual. I thought to myself what the hell, it will not hurt just to call and see if she is still available. Although, a woman like that I know would be taken and swept off her feet by some rich guy. Once again my luck, Alexis was not in any serious relationship and in fact she was looking to date again. I invited Alexis to my place for dinner and a movie. She agreed to come over for me to cook dinner for her and to enjoy a nice love story movie. This time I did not have to convince her to come over for a night cap she was already there. Somehow, I tape half of the love story and half way through the tape was a porno movie. When it came on I act so surprised and embarrassed and upset that I could not believe that they would sell this video to me. But in fact Alexis laugh and said lets watch it. I was hoping she would have said that. I went into the kitchen and came back with a black rose number nine and handed it to her and said this is because you are so beautiful and kind hearted. She smile and smelled the rose and said thank you James. I made love to Alexis all night long but it still did not feel as good as Isabella made me feel. Lord I hope I am not falling in love with Isabella, but I have not been able to get her out of my mind lately. Although, I was here with Alexis, my mind was on Isabella. I was so happy when Alexis had to go because I really wasn't feeling her like that, we had no connection and the sex was average nothing at all to talk about, in fact it was boring. She'll be the first female that I would not be calling again, this is our last night. This female deserved a Black Rose and for the first time in my life I did not have any conscience for giving this rose to her.

Chapter Five

LATER THAT EVENING, I jump up out of bed when I lean over and look at the clock on my end table, I could not believe that I slept this late. It was almost 5 pm and in a couple of hours it will be dark. I did not want the night fall to come and I am home alone. I hate to be home at night alone because of the continue nightmares of Rose in my head, all night long. So I hurry to scramble my clothes together before the night came. I quickly got dressed, put on my loose—fitted blue jeans, red dress shirt, red dress shoes and my blue jean jacket. As I headed in the direction towards the table to grab my keys; I caught a small glimpse of myself in that mirror, with all the anger and hatred that been build up inside of me, all I could see is a dark twisted soul that is eager to find his next victim. I glance down at the answering machine but I was in no mood to check it so I left it blinking. I step out into the hallway, lock the door and rush down the stairs wondering how many single ladies I will be able to convince to come back to my place for a night cap. As I started down the street I heard this loud music playing from the bar down the street so I headed in that direction toward the bar. When I got closer to the bar I was overcome by the music. The Music was pumping and the bar was crowded and packed with beautiful women of all statues. I have never seen so many beautiful women gather in one place. I feel like a child inside of the candy shop. I step inside of the bar and proceed to walk toward the bar to have a seat until I heard a female voice squeaking and yelling out my name. When I turned around to see who this woman was, there stood a slim dark complexion female by the name of Samantha that I went to High School with. She looked incredible and beautiful just as I remember. Last time I heard she had got married to a guy in the military and moved overseas with him. I was so happy to see her; she was one of my closest female friends. Her family use to live right next door to my family. Good lord it's been twenty-five years since I last seen her, she did gain a few pounds, but still very beautiful in the face. We sat at the bar drinking and talking about her being divorced with two kids, unemployed and in college. It was very nice talking to her for an hour but she had to go because she had classes in the morning, so we exchange phone numbers and promised to keep in touch.

After Samantha left I was approached by two beautiful females, one wanted to dance and the other wanted me to join her at her table. I properly declined both female invitations. As I sat there listening to the world of music. I wonder to myself should I be punished. Or should I feel guilty? Living the luxury life is something to be enjoyed. If I'm not calling a chick, then I'm sexing a bitch and giving them something they will regret in a lifetime. I can say I had my share of beauty, smart, ugly and heavy women. Some were innocent others wasn't. My thoughts took over my mind, I no longer heard the music and I kept drinking to suppress my pain and clear my head. The more I drank the more I forgot how much I was hurting and who I was hurting. Then my thought was interrupted by a female asking me if the seat next to me was available, when I turned around I was in total shock I had to blink twice. I could not believe my eyes. There she stood long hair and a tan skin, the more I blink the more she looked like Rose. I look down and my glass was empty. I would have gotten up and beat the hell out of her, but I couldn't stop stumbling. I wanted to give this bitch a piece of my mind. I punched that bitch in her face and she went flying to the floor. I didn't care she deserve an ass whipping of a lifetime so I kick her in the stomach. Before I realize people were holding me back. I just couldn't hold it in no more she's the reason why I am so angry. I had lost it. Just before the police arrive I remember telling the lady "you dirty b-tch, you gave me AIDS and you did not tell me." You said you love me but you gave me no choice to see you rot in hell. You lied to me and now you want to celebrate. You left me here to f-cking die, you stupid b-tch. If I could I would kill you b-tch, f-ck you Rose. I was handcuff and placed in the back of the police car, when I look out the window the women I thought was Rose, was not Rose. I had hit an innocent woman by mistake. But the mark on her face shows how mad I been with Rose. After tonight I realize I am not over her death. That very night I been in bar after bar. The next day I was bailed out of jail by a female named Crystal, the friend of a friend of mine in high school name Samantha. She explained Samantha sent her to bail me out after she had heard what happen. Crystal was this beautiful British girl with a sexy accent. The next day Crystal offered me a ride down to the police station. I had to prove to the police it was my car that was towed. Crystal explained to me that she had to go and will call me later to check up on me to see if everything was okay. I thank her and ask her if I could return the favor by taking her out to eat when her schedule was free. We exchange numbers and the police said that my car was ready for me to walk around and pick it up. The police had escorted me to the back so that I may get my car. On the way there we talked and laughed I could tell that she was flirting with me. She asked me if the woman that dropped me off was my girlfriend or wife. I laugh and said no, my sister, why are you jealous? She laughs and said thank god, I thought she was a drag queen. So you have a friend that I could date better than her, bring it on, I'm single. She said that's funny so am I. 'Oh' by the way my father is having a get together tonight for his Birthday at BBQ, I want you to come! Can you make it? The place is located on West 4th downtown across the street from the little mall on the left. It was 9:30pm when I arrived at BBQ, there was a live band playing and a crowd of people over indulging in alcohol. I spot Jenna in the corner of the room surrounded by four guys. She was totally beautiful in her short black dress that complements her gorgeous body. As I grew closer toward Jenna, I could see that she was in fact dancing and laughing hysterically in the center of the guys. At one point I felt a little jealousy arising inside of me until I realized that it was foolish to be jealous of someone I just met. But she looks amazing dancing and her smile was remarkable. Jenna looks up from dancing and caught my eyes watching her, she smiles and headed quickly in my direction. She throws her arms around me and kisses me on my cheek. Jenna whispers in my ear, "James, I am so happy you came, at first I thought you had changed your mind." She offered me a drink as we mingle, drink and dance. Finally the party was over. Jenna and I exchange numbers; she promised she would call me early next week to set up a second date. When I was headed out the door I realized that I was not ready to go home, so I reach in my pocket and grab my phone and dial Crystal's number hoping she would answer the phone, but instead a young child answers the phone so I figure that was the wrong number so I hung up. But then my phone rang with the number I just called; at first I wasn't going to answer it, afraid it would have been the young child's dad, but it was Crystal. She had said that she was babysitting her niece and did not realize that she had answered her phone. She apologized that she will not be available tonight, but she will call me in the morning and make plans for a date. At one point I felt like I had no choice now but to go home, but everything inside of me screamed I don't want to go home to that dark cold place of hell. As I drove down the street headed to my house, I could see the blinking light from the strip club. I look down at the black rose number 10 laying next to me in the passenger seat that was in fact meant for Jenna if she would have came home with me. I was truly disappointed that she did not come home with me and I hate feeling rejected, in minutes I could feel myself getting angrier and angrier.

I told myself she will pay for rejecting me then I heard a tap on the window it was this man asking if everything is okay, I explain by telling him I just finish a call and I am on my way inside. As I step inside of the strip club, there were several female serving drinks butt naked, one female on the pole dancing and the other giving private lap dances. Damn, it was like a man heaven all the women you want in one place. I went over to the bar at first and request a Black Russian, as I turn around there was a very young but beautiful female who wanted to know if I would like a lab dance. She was too beautiful for me to refuse so I agree to pay for a lap dance. She said her name was "Jessenia" and she been stripping for 5years now. By the way she was dancing you could tell that she had been dancing over 5 years or more. She rubs her big fat ass all over my manhood that I was so rock hard and horny. I whisper in her ear "I wish I could put this big hard penis in you, damn baby you got me so horny" to my surprised she said that if I am willing to pay she could do whatever I want, so we left the strip club to go to my car so I could pull my car around the back where it was dark and turn the car off so I could pull out my penis for Jessenia to show me her talent. Jessenia was sucking my penis like it was a pickle and she did not want the juice to fall, damn she was doing it so good that I could not help but to cum but she swallowed like a pro.

I turn her over and just started f-cking her doggy style instead of vaginal, I went so deep in her ass that it made me incredibly horny then I put it inside of her mouth. I came so hard that my heart was beating so fast that it felt like it was outside of my body. I paid Jessenia and handed her the black rose number 10 that was sitting in my passenger seat as a thank you. First she smiles then became upset when she looks down and realized that I never put on the condom she gave me. She ask me why I didn't use a condom, I told her I honestly forgot and not to worry because she was the only female that I had sex without a condom. I drove Jessenia back around the strip club and I ask her if I could see her again and she agreed. The beeping sound coming from my cell phone let me know that I had a miss call. The miss call was from Jenna letting me know that she had a good time at the BBQ and would like to go out next weekend if I am available. I was so tired from being out all night this week that I finally went home to get some rest.

Chapter Six

THIS WAS THE first time in a long time I woke up with a hang over, I got out of bed and took a long cool shower for some strange reason I felt very hungry. Only wearing my bath towel, I went to my refrigerator and realized there was nothing in there but a piece of bread, one can of beer and the smell of spoil food that seem to have turn my stomach sour. After cleaning out the refrigerator I realized that there was nothing to eat in there, so I went to my room and put my clothes on and headed out the door to the first fast food place I saw. The weather was not too hot but it was just right, as I drove down the street I see people on both sides of the road in their shorts, skirts and tank tops. Watching the kids enjoying the weather laughing and playing without a care in the world, they look so innocent and happy. There I was in the McDonalds drive through; I heard this sweet sexy female voice that interrupted my thoughts, "Welcome to McDonalds can I take your order." When I got to the window I reach for my money without looking I made a remark "I don't mind paying as long as I can have your number" when I look up and realized it was a man with a soft female sexy voice, my face turned red from embarrassment. Then the guy said in his soft spoken voice "I am flattered but I'm taken" I could not wait to get out of McDonalds fast enough that I did not see the car turning in so we collide into each other. A woman jumped out yelling, and then I jump out my car to see if she was alright, she told me she did not see me and she do not have any type of car insurance. I look at my car and there was no damage so I told her not to worry about it and I will take care of my own car but she insists that I take her number just in case something goes wrong with my car after she leaves. I told her that it was not that serious, but if she would like I could have my mechanic take a look at it then we could discuss the damage over dinner tonight and she could bring her brother along. She agreed to have dinner and told me her name was Rosetta but they call her Rose for short. I spend many days and night trying to forget that b-tch Rose just to meet someone else by the name Rosetta. She would like me to call her Rose for short. I forced a fake smile to my lips and said to her "it's a pleasure to meet you," in fact I felt sick to my stomach. When I returned home I was tired so I try to lie down to get some rest for my date tonight with Rosetta. Lately I have been tired a lot I guess it's from having HIV, not getting enough rest and not having any treatment for my HIV. But unfortunately, I toss and turned that whole afternoon because I kept having continued dreams about Rose. I have not dreamed about Rose in over a week. It felt so strange to be going out on a date with a woman with Rose name. I could no longer rest so I got up hoping that if I drink a beer it would relax me and even put me to sleep. That evening it started raining, I knew it was going to be a very nasty night, the rain made it a little bit cold and even made your lips shiver. I was able to make it to the flower shop and the restaurant in plenty of time to reserve us a table and have a drink at the bar before Rosetta arrive. Rosetta finally arrive 45 minutes late to Red Lobster for dinner accompany by her was her brother, she apologize for being late and said, "it's was raining cats and dogs outside, if it was not for the weather she would not have been late." Rosetta and her brother was slightly wet from the rain; she was wearing a two piece white silk skirt outfit with white strap up leg boots and Rodney was wearing a dark blue jeans with a nice shirt that had a flag on it and under the flag was the word Jamaica the name of his country. I smile and said it was not a problem as long as she's safe. Rosetta smile and introduce me to her brother Rodney. I was extremely fascinated by his deep Jamaican accent. Once we were all seated, I hand her the black rose with the number 11 on it, Rosetta was very impressed by my choice of rose. But at the same time, Rodney was examining the rose like he was hired by the school of scientist to study roses. He became very inquisitive about the rose. He wanted to know why I chose a black rose instead of red, what is the meaning for a black rose and what does the number 11 printed on the rose stand for. I was not going to explain myself to no child so I change the subject and started talking about Jamaica the country, which Rodney and Rosetta was very happy to talk about and I enjoyed their memories and places that they thought that I should or should not go see when I go to visit. Rosetta excuse herself from the table to go to the ladies room, leaving me and Rodney alone to talk to each other. After a few minute, Rosetta returned back from the ladies room. James and Rodney was so preoccupied by their conversation that neither one of them noticed that Rosetta was back from the bathroom and had taken her seat until the waitress ask her would she like something to drink and that's when both me and Rodney turn our attention back onto her. Rosetta laughs and said, "What were you men whispering over here about." Both Rodney and I laugh then I excused myself to go to the bathroom but before I left, I lean over to Rosetta and said "Please don't leave until I get back" then off I went in the direction of the bathroom but shortly after Rodney enter inside the bathroom. I heard the sound of the bathroom door being lock when he enters from out of the stool to wash my hand I saw Rodney standing with his back against the door. I was a little on the confused side, I did not know what his intention was, was it to talk or fight. But before I could ask Rodney what was wrong, he pushes me against the wall then whispers in my ear, "I know you were flirting with me and we both know you want me." I was so confused by Rodney statement because I had no idea what Rodney was talking about because all I knew was that he was just trying to be nice to me because of his sister. So when I tried to explain Rodney pushes him against the wall again, but this time he unzip my pants pull out my manhood and begin to put his mouth over my manhood giving me head. It was feeling so good that I did not stop or push him away and just before I was about to cum there was a knock on the door from a customer trying to use the bathroom, I quickly ran inside of the stool to fit my clothing while Rodney open the door and returned back to his seat with his sister to wait for me to come from the bathroom to eat. Finally when I returned back to the table looking a little on the pale side, I apologized for making them wait by explaining that I had an important business phone call that I had to take. At first, I felt a little bit uneasy until Rodney started to tell jokes breaking the tension between us as if what happen in the bathroom never happen and because I did not want Rosetta to question me about anything. I played along like everything was normal but made no eye contact with Rodney. I manage to keep all my focus on Rosette as we talk and laugh all through dinner until it was time for Rosetta to go, we had to have been there for almost two and a half hours. She and Rodney both thank me for dinner and said they both had a good time. I escorted them to their car, as Rodney was getting into the car turn around and said, "James, you never told me what the black rose meant and the number on it." I thought by all the conversation we had that he would have forgotten about the rose. I had to play it off so I laugh and said it means unity and 11 years of friendship. Rosetta laughed while Rodney had this puzzle look on his face as they drove off. I went back inside of Red lobster sat at the bar and order a White Russian to drink. I waited 30 minute until I was sure that she and Rodney both were well inside of the house before I called her. I told her that I was just checking that she got home safe. While I waiting for AAA at Red Lobster because my car had broke down, she insisted that she come and give me a ride home since I been good to her and her brother. By the time she did arrive, I was on the intoxicated side; this time she came alone. As we approach the house, I offered Rosetta to come in and have a quick drink with me but she politely declined and said it was late. Then I ask for her to help me into the house at the same time pleading with her to have one drink with me for my birthday after several pleases she agrees to have one drink and leave after that. So she opens the door for me and escorted me onto the couch. I pulled her down on top of me and she look in total shock and tried to gain her balance but my weight over powered hers. She said in a scared and shaky voice, "James I have to go." When I told her I would not let her go, fear rose on her face, her eyes grew bigger as if she saw a ghost as she tried to ease her body from under me. I beg for her to stay the night with me, just to lie down next to me and we don't even have to have sex. Rosetta explained that she was not comfortable to spending the night but she will stay to have a couple of drinks and then she really have to be going. I told her I respected her choice not to stay the night with me at this time then I let her go. I brought her a glass of wine for us to toast, we talked and laugh for hours and I kept pouring Rosetta a glass of wine until she was on the intoxicated side, on her last glass of wine I drop in an E pill. She thanked me again and said that she really needs to be going, I told her let me use the bathroom and then I would walk her out to the car. When I came back from the bathroom and stood in the entrance of the living room, I could see Rosetta sitting on the couch butt naked moaning and playing with her vagina like a cat in heat. As I watch from the doorway my manhood begins to get so hard and I was so horny that I wanted to just ram my hard rock manhood up in her. She did not realize that I was watching her, while she continues to play with her breast and vagina. I finally walk over to the couch as if I was in total shock, and said to her "Rosetta what are you doing? Girl, stop playing and get dress." Rosetta looked up from what she was doing but never one time stop playing with her vagina to say, "James, I want you, I am so horny; then just let me ride it." I could tell that the pill was working and Rosetta was totally horny and I can't wait to give it to her, my big, 10 inch rock hard manhood. I could tell Rosetta wanted it by the way she pulled me on top of her. I was never the type to like easy girls and Rosetta was turning me on. I had to play it off that I did not want sex from her, so again I said, "Rosetta, what are you doing? You don't want me so stop all this foolish talk and get dress" Rosetta act as if she did not hear me and continue to play with herself at the same time talking sexually and dirty to me. She grabs my hand and places it between her legs so I could see how wet she was. Then she started to undo my pants to stroke my manhood up and down, I jump up off the couch and told her that I was going to make her some coffee to help get some of the alcohol out of her system. She follows me into the kitchen and then she said, "I know you want this wet tight vagina, I could feel how hard your manhood is, come on let's just f-ck unless James are you gay?" I said, "Hell No" as I pour another glass of wine and slip another pill inside of it because I did not want the first pill to wear off, and then I pour a cup of coffee I knew that Rosetta would not have chosen the coffee. I hand her the cup of coffee, she refused and reached for the wine instead which I knew she was going to do. I told her that she did not need that wine she needed coffee, but she drunk the wine in one swallow and then she said "James all I need is you and for you to give me that big rock in your pants." She started undoing my belt, button and zipper; I said, "No Rosetta" but I could not get the rest of the words out of my mouth before Rosetta started pressing her soft sweet lips against mine. She was kissing my lips hungry like she did not eat in years, then she push me down on the chair after rubbing my manhood until it was hard as a rock finally she sat on my manhood and started riding it up and down, back and forth fast and slow as she fools around with her vagina moaning louder and louder. Her vagina was so tight and wet that it was making me crazy and wanting her more and more. Finally I could not control it was like an animal inside of me being wakened from a sleep. I pick Rosetta up and put her on the table started f--king the hell out of her then I turn her over put it in her ass, she moan and plead for more. I fucked harder and harder and deeper and deeper, I pick her up and f--ked her while I walk her over to the couch. Rosetta looks as if she was still hungry for my manhood so I put it in her mouth and she suck, lick and kiss all over my manhood. I stick it inside her ass again and started to f--k her doggy style then we assumed the 69 position and last I exploded in her vagina after Rosetta let out a cry of total satisfactory we passed out.

Chapter Seven

I **WOKE UP TO** a woman sobbing, I could not remember last night for nothing so I could not understand why Rosetta was crying. She was curled up in a ball and sobbing in her hand uncontrollable like she had just lost her whole life. I got up and stumble over to Rosetta with my head still pounding from a hangover. I place my hand on her shoulder to comfort her, but she pulls back and looked at me with eyes red as blood and with her lips turned up she said in a cold freezing angry voice, "don't touch me" so I said, "Rosetta what's wrong with you." She said "LIKE YOU DON'T KNOW, YOU DRUGED ME AND RAPED ME JAMES." I said, "I did no such thing Rosetta and stop telling those lies." You came home with me on your own. I did not force you to go out with me on a date or come back to my house. The truth be told you came on to me like the prostitute you are, and you know I did not rape you. You are just trying to hide what a prostitute you are. Then she busted out yelling, "LIAR, I CAN'T BELIEVE YOU DID THIS TO ME. YOU DID DRUG ME AND RAPE ME. YOU ARE NOTHING BUT A LIAR AND YOU WILL PAY FOR THIS." She threw the bottle of E pills at me. I was so mad, I told her that I hate when dirty ass young girls try to act like a women and that she didn't come over to play cards or Barbie doll so she knew what she was doing and nobody raped her and it was all in her head. And for her not to play that bull shit rape game. I am a grown ass man who does not need to rape anyone. I told her to get the hell out. She started screaming at the top of her lungs, "Forget You James." I'll kill you and then she ran into the kitchen. When she returned, she was holding a knife in her right hand, she drop the knife then told me that I was not worth it and she was going to the police station to file rape charges against me. I got very upset then I grab her arm and told her that I will kill her if she goes to the police with that lie when the truth was you slept with me in exchange for not fixing my car because you had no insurance. In fact you seduced me so you will not have to pay to fix my car and when I ask you for my money to fix my car you started screaming rape that's what I will tell the police. You were no more than a prostitute, and it was my word against hers. She looks at me in amazement and shock that I would tell that story to make her look like a prostitute. I told her to get her sorry ass out of my house. I proceeded to walk over in the direction towards the door to open it so I could escort her out of my apartment. As Rosetta was walking towards the door she flipped over the coffee table, pushed the computer monitor onto the floor along with the speakers, mouse and other important items. Next she threw the wine glasses in the direction towards me barely missing me by an inch but manage to hit my mirror forcing it to break and shatter making a mess all over the floor. Just before I could stop her, she threw the television remote control at the TV cracking the screen. Finally she stormed out of my apartment slamming the door so hard that it flew back open and mange to knock off the wall, the only picture I had left of Rose and shattered into thousands of tiny pieces. At the same time yelling and screaming over her shoulder running down the hallway passing the doors saying, "She's going to make me pay for raping her." Forcing the neighbors to exit out of their apartments to see what all the commotion is about. When I glanced over to the door I noticed that my neighbors were in the hallway looking in and whispering to each other as they walk pass. I walk over to the door with my cheeks being red from embarrassment. I apologized to my neighbors for the disturbance and then I shut my door. As I look around to see what my neighbors were looking, pointing and whispering among each other over how my house was a complete mess from being destroyed by Rosetta. All I could say is, "why me, why as if I didn't have enough problems" I started cleaning up my apartment then I noticed a couple of drops of blood on the couch and a trail of blood on the living room floor leading into the kitchen. It finally came to me that this was Rosetta blood and last night was her first time. She never been with a man before, she was in fact a virgin. I felt completely bad and ashamed. How could I have forced myself on this young lady, putting an E pill in her drink? The first time in a long time my conscience got the best of me. I have to stop doing this to these females who did not do anything to me it was Rose and she's dead and I should not make anyone else suffer for Rose mistake from this day on. I am done spreading the virus and I will get treatment. As I continue to think about what I did to Rosetta I felt a pain in the pit of my stomach. I was sick to my stomach. I tried to make some kind of sense out of it like her performance last night made me feel as if it was like she knew what she was doing and knew what she wanted, but the truth be told, it was just the E pill I gave her to make her act like that. I felt even worse the more I thought about it. I had to get out of my apartment. I needed a drink hoping it will help me forget about what I did to Rosetta. But when I step outside my car was nowhere to be found, at first I thought someone had stolen it. Then I remember that I left it at Red Lobster last night and Rosetta brought me home in her car. As I glance down at my clock and noticed how late it was getting, I realized I needed to get to Red Lobster. I called a cab and once it arrived I got inside headed in the direction towards the restaurant until I heard my cell phone ring inside my left pocket. I reached inside with a delay glance at the phone and looked at the caller ID then noticed that was Crystal. At first I did not want to answer my phone, but I did on the other end of the receiver was Crystal asking if I would like company. At first I wanted to decline the invitation, until I remembered about the doctor appointment I have in the morning. At that moment I felt like it would be a good idea for Crystal to come over as a distraction. Since tomorrow morning would be the first day of my treatment and tonight I just wanted to forget about my sickness and live a normal life. As soon as I pulled up to the apartment, Crystal's car was already parked there and she was standing outside of her car waiting. I immediately got out of the car both Crystal and I walked towards each other and once we were close enough, I wrapped my arms around her squeezing her close against my chest and gave her a big bear hug. As I whisper in her ear, " you are truly so beautiful, I don't want to let you go." Crystal just laughs as she eases slowly out of my arms and took my hand and led me upstairs to my apartment. She took my keys out of my hand to open the door and playfully pushed me inside of my apartment then quickly closed the door. Once the door was locked she escorted me by my hand over to the couch, pushing me down on it then walked away to the kitchen just to return with two glasses and a wine bottle as if this was her house. After she poured the wine into the glasses she handed it to me and with the other one she place it on the table until she turn down the lights. She turned on some soft music making it an incredible romantic evening. I felt that it could not be any more incredible, until she returns and stood right in front of me. She opened up her coat and to my surprise she was completely nude. Without even a word she removed the glass of wine from my hand then placed it on the table and began kissing all over me, as she unfastened my belt buckle and unzipped my pants exposing my big manhood as she sucked on it nice and slow causing me to close my eyes and murmur in pleasure after a couple of minutes. Crystal climbed on top of me and began to ride my manhood as she was taking complete control. It felt like we made love for eternity just before we both passed out from exhaustion. When I woke up I glanced over and saw Crystal sleeping so peaceful like an angel that I did not want to wake her up. So I left her a note saying that I would return back in an hour; left breakfast next to the bed on the night stand a long with a black rose with a gold number 12 on it, and for her to make herself at home.

Chapter Eight

IT FELT AS if I had been at the doctor's office for 8 hours, but I only been here for two hours. I had to fill out some paper work listing everybody I had sex with since I am being treated for this virus. I had to have a full checkup, blood work, and some counseling by a social worker then finally; I pick up my medication from the pharmacy, now I am on my way home. I was totally exhausted being at the doctor's office. As I put the keys in the door, I just remember that I left Crystal lying in the bed. So I stuck the pills deep down inside of my pocket, fix my clothes, open the door and headed into my bedroom to greet her. But to my surprise she was not there instead there was a note on the dresser written in her beautiful letter cover in sweet smelling perfume scent, thanking me for a wonderful night, breakfast and a beautiful rose. Then said that she really had a great time and she was sorry that she had to leave for work, but she would call me later. I was so happy that Crystal was not there because my body was aching all over that I had no choice but to take my medication and lay down to get some rest. I know for me to get some rest I would have to turn off the ringer on my cell phone and the house phone then turn my answering machine down as well to not be disturbed. It felt like I have been sleeping all day. I finally woke up the next evening round 6pm, my body felt so much better from resting. I still have not accepted that I have HIV and it was making my body get tired quicker and when they asked me to list all the names of the females that I had slept with on the doctor's form, I only listed one person that bitch Rose who gave it to me. Everybody else is on their owned, as I laughed to myself. This was the first time, in a long time I was home alone, and I was finally enjoying being by myself. I was no longer afraid being alone and I was not sexing anyone or handing out roses. I was just resting, not even bothered by my conscience or guilt finally I found peace after all these months. I was no longer angry or mad at the world. In fact, I no longer had the need to hurt anyone else or hand out any more roses. Today is the first day I felt alive and wanted to live and was not being haunted by Rose memories. It was as if I had been set free to live and be happy. I did not realize that it's been three weeks since I been out with a female or to a party, I was able to catch up on some paper work, house work, rest and relax in total peace. I truly dread turning on my cell there were five miss calls, four voice messages was from Crystal and one was from Gina. When I turn on my house phone to check the answering machine two calls from my mother and seven urgent calls from an officer by the name Detective Miller asking me to give him a call or come down to the station because he need to speak to me concerning some serious matter then he left his number and the other 10 calls were telemarketers trying to sell me something I don't need. I called my mother back first since she was not at home I left a message on my mother's answering machine, letting her know I was okay but just busy. When I called the Detective back I was so nervous and confused to why detective Miller needed to talk with me. I dialed the number with my finger shaking and scared to death if he answers, but he did not answer so I let out a sign of relief when I heard his voicemail saying he will be out of the office for one week and will return all calls when he returns so I left a message on the Officer machine and quickly hung up, and then erased the rest of my messages. Then I called Crystal back, she started to explain to me that she had been feeling sick or a couple of days and she has an appointment to see her doctor next week and she really would like me to come with her. She said that she is so scared that she may be pregnant and that I was the only man she been with so she knows that I am the father. When I heard doctor, pregnant and I am the father my mind and body went numb and limp. I felt like I had a rock stuck in my throat and I needed a drink of water and the floor was removed right from under my feet. I need to sit down. All I could think about is Crystal finding out that she has HIV and is pregnant at the same time. I felt something in the pit of my stomach, how could I have done this evil thing to my unborn child, what kind of monster would hurt an unborn baby? That same peace I had before I called Crystal turn into shock, fear, anger and then once again pure rage. An innocent child is going to pay for what I did, no not just any child my child. The tears rolled down the side of my cheek. What have I done, I have become my worst nightmare. I have always wanted a child of my own ever since I was dating Rose. When Rose had got sick at first I was so excited because I was hoping that she was sick because she was pregnant but instead the bitch lied and said she had cancer and I was so determined to be there for her throughout all her treatment. She had me looking like a fool when she knew all along she had AIDS. I guess the joke was on me. I was so deep in thought that I forgot Crystal was still on the phone until I heard her call out my name and ask if I was still on the phone I answer, "Yes I am

Love" she asked me to go with her to her doctor appointment, the words seem to stumble out of my mouth S—ure. I would be happy to go with you, just let me know when, where, and what time your appointment is next week. She thanks me for being very supportive and not getting upset then she hung up. After hanging up with Crystal, I felt so lost, confused and did not know what to do. My shaking was uncontrollable as if I had a shaking syndrome. I was so scared like a five year old child who just watched a scary movie by themselves. The first time in a long time I felt like praying not for myself but for my baby if she turned out to be pregnant. I got down on my knees and started praying the phone rang. I jump up fast to pick up the phone thinking it would be Crystal calling back saying it was a false alarm she's not pregnant and her period came. It was a man on the other end of the phone yelling, shouting and threatens to kill me. At first, I thought maybe he had the wrong phone number and was about to hang up then he said James, you will pay for raping my sister. Rosetta did not deserved what you did to her. You drugged her, got her drunk then raped her. I will hunt you down and kill you; that is a promise then he slam the phone down before I could respond back. Then when the phone rang again I knew it was Rosetta brother Rodney calling back but this time I was ready to give him a piece of my mind and let him know that I am not scared of anyone and if it is a fight he want then it will be a fight to the death. So when I pick up my phone I started yelling into the receiver, "Listen here Rodney; I'm only going to say this one time, what happened between Rosetta and I have nothing to do with you and if you call my phone one more time, I will drive to your house and beat the hell out of you." Just as I was about to slam the phone down, I heard a woman yell my name, "James, James", and this time on the other end of the phone turn out to be Gina. "Hello James," this is Gina; "sorry if I caught you at a bad time would you like for me to call you back on another day?" My face turns red from embarrassment hearing her voice. I apologized to her and told her it's never a bad time whenever she called me. She laughs and I laugh, we talk for an hour nonstop. I could tell by the conversation that Gina seems to be a take charge, very strong dominate female. Then she asked me if I had dinner yet and she was hungry and haven't had anything to eat since lunch so she invited me to join her for dinner on the beach at a restaurant. I hesitated at first to say yes because I wanted to decline and tell her that I was too tired to go out but my stomach was growling so loud, then I thought I could use a night out to forget about Crystal and Rodney both. I heard Gina voice, "James, are you still there?" I answer with my voice slightly on the shaky side. "Yes, Sweetie I am still here," then Gina said "I ask you if you was free to have dinner with me, I had a really bad week and really would like to forget about it and have some fun for once." At that moment I truly understood how Gina felt, so I told her I would love to have dinner with her tonight. She said that she will meet me at the restaurant by the beach in two hours, and for me to dress casual so I could be comfortable when we walk on the beach after dinner; she giggled and then hung up.

Chapter Nine

AS I RUMBLE through my clothes to figure out what should I put on, that will totally impress Gina enough that she would not be able to take her eyes off me. I pulled out my brown and black Stacey Adam two piece outfit from the closet along with my Stacey Adam brown shoes with black tips. Next I headed into the bathroom to take a shower; soon after the shower I could feel the pain all over my body as if I had been hit by a pickup truck so I reach for my pills. I still cannot believe that I have HIV and it only had been two weeks since I started this treatment. I glance over at the time and saw how late it was getting so I took a deep breath and continue getting dress as fast as I could, took a quick glance in the mirror. The minute the cool breeze brush across my face, I knew tonight was a perfect night for a walk on the beach after dinner. I waited outside of the restaurant inside my car for Gina to arrive so together we could enter into the restaurant. Finally, Gina arrived 10 minutes late, we headed towards the restaurant walking hand in hand then stopping for a moment to look up at the stars. The moon was full tonight it peeped at us as if it was looking at itself in the ocean. The breeze was magnificent and peaceful. The music was an excellent addition, very soft and pleasant to our ears as the waitress directed us to our seat on the deck overlooking the beach a candle light lit at every table. The deck was full of people's laughter circling the air, Gina looked beyond gorgeous in her white and gold dress that cling tight around every curve of her body with gold shoes. Gina has a natural beauty but the make up tonight just enhanced her beauty even more. She was totally stunning with her hair pull back in a bun out of her face. I could hardly keep my eyes off of her, just then music from the live band started playing; a tall man grab the microphone and started to sing a Michael Bolton song "When a Man Loves a Woman," I took Gina by the hand escorted her on to the dance floor. I wrap my arm around her waist, pulled her slightly against my chest, stared into her eyes and place my lips over hers planting a soft gentle kiss on her lips. I was so happy when the music came to an end because I could feel my manhood rise and I did not want to be embarrassed returning to my table with my penis at attention. Gina smiles and said, "James, I am really having a wonderful time, thank you for making this night incredible." I smiled at how astonishing she looks tonight; we laugh and talk; I got to know where Gina grew up and about her family. Gina did entirely most of the talking and it did not bother me at all because I did not have to talk about myself. She talked about how she was married once, now divorced, no kids and love her job and family. In the near future she would love to get married again and have kids. But for now her job is too demanding of her time. After a long period of time, the waitress interrupted our conversation by introducing herself to us by saying, "Hi my name is Patricia and I will be your waitress for tonight." "I apologized for nobody coming over to take your drink order because this place has been packed but if you are ready to order, I will be happy to take your order now." Gina did not hesitate to order her drink and meal, as a gentleman I order my drink and meal after her. The waitress disappeared to put our order in then return with our drinks and some bread with butter for us to eat until our food was ready. I forgot all about the rose I brought for Gina, so I reached down under the table pull out a bag with a dozen of roses in it and hand it to her, the roses consists of three red roses, three white roses, three yellow roses, three pink roses and one black rose with gold trim round it, engrave with the number 13 on it. Gina was so overwhelm by the roses, she had tears in her eyes "James the roses are beautiful, thank you" she reached over to kiss me on the lips, then she said "James, why is there one black rose mix in with the rest of the roses and what does this black rose stand for?" I laugh out loud; kiss her on both hands afterward I said, "Sweetheart, there is no such thing as a black rose. It's a dark purple but in this light it looks black and this rose symbolizes the beginning of a new friendship" she laughs and said, "I like that James, a new beginning" Subsequently, she started asking me so many questions about the roses as if she was a reporter. I started to get nervous and a little agitated. So, I change the subject by kissing her lips and telling her how lovely she looks and I could not resist kissing her. Thank god, the food arrives because I was running out of ideas to divert her attention from the roses. At one point I wish I never gave her the roses. Then we talk about the most embarrassing stupid thing we did in our young adult life. Once again our conversation was interrupted by the waitress asking us if we needed our drinks refilled and she was leaving for the evening, another waitress will be over to bring out our drinks and at that time she will also take our dessert order. She wished us a good evening then turned and walked away. We continue our conversation; I smile the whole time because all I could think about is how beautiful Gina look in the candle light and the moon reflecting off her face together making her look even more exquisite. Just looking at her made me want to kiss her again and hold her in my arms all night if it was only possible, so I said to Gina, "You have something on your lips, and will you give me the honor of kissing it off those beautiful sexy lips." She responded in a playful tone by saying, "why, Mr. James, are you trying to get fresh with me." I answer her by saying. "No Sweetie I am a true gentleman, I just don't want the food on your lips to overpower your beauty and I am trying to be your knight and rescue your beautiful lips from the food. Women always cry about how they want a hero, now I am trying to be a hero and you will not let me be your hero and rescue those lips from danger." Gina laughs hysterically out loud, her tears roll down her cheek while she was holding her stomach to maintain her posture. After a short period of time, she was able to pull herself together and said, "Since you said it that way, what girl does not want a hero. I said, "Come here baby" pulling her chair close in front of me. It started out as a peck on the lips and out of nowhere it got hot and intense, we both forgot that we were in a restaurant instead of in a hotel. The clapping out loud from the crowd of people as the band finish their song scared both Gina and I, then we remember that we were still in the restaurant then we laugh. As the band started playing again some people were getting up to dance, some was eating while others were walking toward the stage to listen to the music up close. Gina said, "James, you have me so hot and horny right now" while she rubs my manhood, I rub her round onion shape butt which fit in the palm of my hand. She whisper in my ear "Go with me to the bathroom" before I could open up my mouth she took my hand and lead me toward the unisex restroom. Everyone seem to be enjoying the music, dancing, talking, singing and the restaurant that was lit by candlelight which made it dark enough for anybody to notice Gina and I walk into the bathroom together. Being very aggressive she pushed me against the bathroom door, unbuttoning my shirt kissing and licking me all over my chest down to my belly. She was licking all the right spots, and then I ran my hand up her dress, good lord! Have mercy! Gina had no panties on and her vagina was dripping wet. She unzips my pants and her hand was stroking my manhood long and gentle. Her hand felt soft as if she had put Vaseline all over them and rub it over my manhood; Gina was begging me to put my manhood in her vagina, so I thrust my manhood inside her vagina hard which made Gina hold me tight while letting out a loud squeal. I started stroking her vagina with my finger while I thrust my manhood in and out her vagina going deeper and deeper inside until I heard Gina whisper in my ear,

"Oh god, James, Oh god, I am about to cum," then she started moaning and shaking with pleasure that I could no longer control myself that I bust so hard that I started groaning; my legs started shaking and the room felt like it was spinning out of control, I thought I was going to pass out but instead I slightly stumble backward. We clean ourselves up and walk back to the table holding hands unnoticed, music was still playing and the dance floor was crowded with people having a great time. Gina laughs and said, "I work up an appetite, now I am ready for dessert and a drink." I laugh and said, "You work up an appetite, last time I check I did all the work and you just enjoyed the ride." We both laugh then Gina wave her hand to signal for the waitress to come over to take her order. I pulled her chair closer to me then told her, she was too far away for me to kiss her beautiful lips and I would love for her to spend the night. I promised her if she comes home with me tonight that I would give her a full body massage, rub her feet, make her a bubble bath, and eat her vagina until she has multiple orgasms and make love to her until daylight. Gina said, "How could I refuse a once in a life time opportunity like that." then agreed to come back home with me. This night was going totally perfect nothing could ruin this night for me. I felt like I am on cloud nine, then I reach over to kiss Gina once again passionately on the lips; eventually, the waitress walks over and said, "Hi, my name is Crystal; I will be your waitress for the rest of the evening. I will be happy to take your order will you need something to drink or have some dessert tonight. In the same breath she gasps and she said, "James?" before I could answer Gina said, "James, do you know this waitress?" I was in total shock that when I open my mouth to respond nothing came out as if I lost my ability to talk right at that moment both my tongue and vocal cords was paralyzed; my face was so pale as if I saw a ghost. All I could think about is Crystal should have been at home in bed since she said she was sick and maybe pregnant with my child. Crystal continue to speak, "I guess you are going to act like you don't know me, right or are you surprised to see me? Of course you are James; you did not know this is my second job I work at because you never asked me what I do or where I work because all I was to you was someone you wanted to sleep with and nothing else." Gina repeated the question, "James! Did you hear me I ask you if you knew this waitress? And you said nothing." Since, I refused to respond because I was still in shock. Gina turns her questions toward the waitress and asked Crystal, "can you tell me how you know James?" Crystal said, "I'm sorry Ms. for destroying your date; James is my baby daddy" as she touches and rubs her stomach, she gasps again saying, "How beautiful" looking down on the table at the roses, next she said, "I guess you are the lucky woman all I got was one black rose with gold trim around it and engraved with the number 12 on it." But then she looks at the roses again and said, "Wait a minute it's just like this one" reaching down on the table and picking out the black rose in the mix with the rest of the roses. She drops it as soon as she saw the 13 engraved on it. In shock she yelled "James her black rose has a number 13 on it! What the hell is going on James?" Gina stood up and slapped the hell out of me, then turned to storm away but I beg her not to leave but to allowed me to explain what's going on. "All I need is 10 minutes of your time." She agreed to only give me 10 minutes and not a minute more. At that moment Crystal returned with our drink and apologized to Gina for ruining her evening but she think she needed to be told the truth. I asked Gina if she could please give Crystal and I one minute to talk this out first then I will finish our conversation after. I lean over to kiss Gina on the lips, she pull her chair back to avoid my kiss then excused herself from the table and headed toward the restroom she said without looking back, "You have five minutes."

Chapter Ten

FROM WHERE I was sitting, I could see Gina exiting out of the restroom to return back to her seat, Crystal was running pass her with tears in her eyes Gina stop her and ask her was she okay, she glance over her shoulder in passing and whisper in her ear crying to Gina, "I am so sorry" as she pass by her. Gina said as soon as she reaches the table, "James, what did you do to that girl?" I smile and said, "Don't worry about her; we just came to an understanding." I explained to Gina that Crystal and I went out once a long while ago and she and I was done but she insist on holding on to this relationship. She even tried telling me that she is pregnant to make me stay but when I ask for documentation she always has 100 excuses why she do not have one. So I told Crystal that I will be willing to go with her to the doctor appointments and she still made excuses why she does not need me to go, she is all about games. I am sorry if this drama ruin our night and for the black roses which is dark blue that mean friendship and I would love for you to remember this night when we both found true love, so everyone I gave a rose to meant something to me. It meant for me true love and forever friendship. I ask her if she would forgive me and finish this night out with me. I told her that I would really like to see where our friendship goes from here. That I am really feeling her and do not want it to end like this. Just then another song came on this time it was a Luther Vandross song 'Here and Now', I reach my hand out to Gina, place her hand in mine, please dance with me. I pull her close again to my chest, smelled her hair, it smells like a combination of strawberry and hot chocolate mixed. Then I stared into her eyes bend down and kiss her lips, her neck then after that I whisper in her ears, "I still want to take you home with me. Come on let's get out of here, come home with me, I need to be with you, to smell you, kiss you and make love to you." James knew that he had a special kind of gift, of always knowing how to smooth talk and convince a female to see things his way every since he was a child. He always been able to make people believe what he was saying was the true gospel. That's why he was able to convince Gina into coming home with him. We dance to Usher 'There goes my baby' then Baby Face 'Whip appeal.' After the Baby Face song I was ready to go home and take

Gina with me before she has time to change her mind. This night was perfect from this point on. I reach to take Gina's hand so we can head out of the door. Then two Officers enter the restaurant and preceded in our direction, all I could think about is what now. They stop right in from of Gina and me. One Officer held a short and brief conversation with Gina. Then turn toward me and said, "Are you James Sinclair." I answered, yes then they turn back around to Gina and apologized for what they have to do. Finally they said to me, "James Sinclair, you are under arrest for the raping of Rosetta Edward. You have the right to remain silent. Anything you say will be used against you in a court of law. You have the right to an attorney during interrogation, if you cannot afford an attorney, one will be appointed to you." Please place your hand behind your back. Gina pleads for them not to arrest me inside of the restaurant and for them to allow her to escort me out with them into the cop car. She said that she will go home change and come down to see how she could help. As soon as they place me into the cop car; turn on the sirens as the rain beat hard against the police windows as if it was trying to break them. I could hear the police officer on his radio calling in my code 130.30. I arrive at the booking station. The back door popped wide open and an officer poked his head inside and said, "Mr.

Sinclair, it's time to go, please step out the vehicle." Then he escorted me inside the station. Once we were in the building he removed the handcuffs then asked me to empty my pockets out, just in case I had a weapon. As I reach inside my pocket to empty it, I pull out my wallet, keys, and loose change. Then my hand came across the bottle of pills that I forgot that I had. At first, I hesitated to pull it out until the officer said, "Mr. Sinclair we are waiting on you to completely empty your pockets." So I handed them the bottle of pills, they whisper amongst each other as they read the label on bottle as they escorted me inside the cell. That night the cell was full with people ready to be process in or release on bond. I was so confused and angry because I did not know how I got to this point. I was being charged with rape. I hear some people complaining about how they were not guilty and others acting as if they were okay about being here. Then there was some laughing and singing like this was a joke. I sat over on the bench and waited until it was my time to be process in. I tried to get comfortable but it was so cold and so loud with all the talking between cell mates and the officer yelling outside of the cage, the open and closing of the cell doors as it slam shut every time it open and closed. There was music playing on top of the desk of the Booking Officer; on the radio, it was playing Jennifer Hudson song

'Giving myself over to you,' this was the first time that I ever listen to the words, and I thought about Rose. I smile because I knew what it truly felt like to have been in love that much. Then anger started to rise inside of me when the song came to an end and I realized why I am in this mess because of Rose. I heard my name being called and the cell door opening for me to exit out. I walked toward an officer that escorted me into the nurse station area, who drawn my blood and test me for TB. I was put in a line to be process in. I was finger printed and had my picture which some call a mug shot. I was given an orange jumpsuit with the word inmate on the back. And told to change my clothes and place them in the bag that I was given. I was given a box with one thin blanket, two white T shirts, one pair of flip flops, one pair of socks, a small bag of personal hygiene stuff in a travel pack size and maybe one or two other stuff that I could not remember at this time. I was then placed among the population of inmates. They explain the rules and regulations at the same time they inform me that I was schedule to see the judge in the morning. The air condition was up so high that the air went straight through this thin blanket. I tried to get comfortable on this hard cot they call a bed. My body started to ache, at that moment I wish I had my pills to stop the pain with it being this cold it made the pain worse. It became so unbearable to get any sleep at all. Looking around this small cell that they call a room with a bare door, no window, a single sink near a toilet and open for everyone to watch you use it. There was no type of privacy, and a small metallic frame with a worn out mattress they called a bed with a thin blanket and everything else was a blur. I could hardly see because the room was slightly lit up by the light from the officers desk and the air condition was turn up so high that I thought I was going to freeze to death, I could not get comfortable at all on this small cot like bed then there was no pillow to elevate my head above my feet. I even had to bend my knees to be able to fit on this cot to go to sleep. Then to make matters worse they deliberately gave me this thin blanket that did not keep me warm at all. I shivered and shake all-night trying hard to forget how cold it was so I could fall asleep. Right now I wish I was home in my bed watching TV or listening to music until I fell asleep but in here there is no TV. I don't know how this does not bother some people to live like this. It's like a cruel punishment not fit for a human. It was also hard for me to sleep since I have been so worried about seeing the judge in the morning and just as soon as I closed my eyes I hear an Officer yelling, "James Sinclair it time for you to see the judge now." The officer handcuffs me and escorted me out of my cage along with a few other inmates that was also schedule to see the judge. We was all place inside of a prison van, transported in handcuffs and leg irons on our feet as well as being chain to each other heading to the courts house. When we enter the court house it was if the judge had an attitude problem. He was yelling and shouting at the inmates giving them all high bails and bonds and long jail sentences as if he hated his job and anyone who committed a crime was guilty. I waited for the Judge to sentence and set the bail bond for the other inmates until he got to my name. Finally, he called my name; I was not worried at all because I knew this was my first offense and no matter how much bail or bond he set, I had enough money. I looked around the court room and saw my mother, Gina, Rosetta and eleven other females holding a black rose inside of their hand. And now this started to worry me again, why are they all here, what has Rosetta done? And why does each female sit with a black rose in their hands? It's a mystery to me, and then I heard the judge call my name again. The judge asked me to rise for the hearing of what I had been charged for as soon as he said, "Mr. James Sinclair you are being charged with the rape of Rosetta Edwards." The court house secretary came in and handed the judge a type document and there was some whispering between the secretary and the judge then she walks out of the court room. The judge looks down at the documentation as if he was speed reading it, he apologize for the interruption to the court. Mr. James Sinclair you have been charged with two accounts, now the first one is the raping of Rosetta Edward and the second is contempt murder by having unprotected sex with 13 females. Knowing that you have the HIV virus and spreading it. Would you like to say something on your behalf to the court? Or make an apology to these females and their family, at first I stood up to apologize to each and every female that I hurt and their family but as I look across the room I saw how I truly hurt these females and they truly did not deserve this punishment that I had given them. So I open my mouth to say I am sorry but when I seen Rodney, Rosetta's brother I wanted to jump over the table and give him a serious beat down, so instead of apologizing I let my anger get the best of me. I blame each and every one of them for being a prostitute. For sleeping with a man they just met unprotected. And then I said if anyone was to blame it would be my ex girlfriend Rose who gave it to me and died without telling me, leaving a gift for me to pass the love around. I smile and laugh then said, "I could apologize for this and by the way ladies I will not be dying alone. Happy Birthday ladies," the judge bang his hammer on the desk over five times to get order back in the court and ask the bailers to escort me back to my jail cell until he was ready to hand down my sentence. As I was being dragged out by the deputies, I was still shouting, "I have no remorse, my legacy will live forever and I will not be dying alone; my way of getting God's attention by getting even with his people." The court door opens as I was escorted out in handcuffs back to my cell, the officer press the elevator button for us to go down to the basement parking lot; for transporting all prisoners back to prison safely without any of the officers being ambushed by a Prisoners' accomplice. I heard someone yelling out my name so I quickly turn around to see who it was. Rodney walks in front of me, his eye pupils was dark and his voice was cold as he opens his mouth to say, "I promised you that I will make you pay." Then he reached inside of his coat, pull out a 44 caliber pistol. He aim it at me his hand was shaking terribly, a snickering laughter escape my mouth because I did not believed he would shoot me. I poked my chest out to taunt him and said, "You are nothing but a punk, you are not going to shoot anybody so put it down and go home to your mother, little boy, this is a man's game." Then I went on to say to Rodney "What you mad I did not give you a black rose but not to worry I gave you a gift that you could never give back, H.I.V, the gift that keeps on giving; now you can die along with me, I hope it was worth your life." Then he started laughing trying to make Rodney mad enough to pull the trigger to kill him so he would not have to die in jail but when he saw Rodney was hesitating about pulling the gun and he was having second thoughts he tried once again to make Rodney mad enough by saying, "Did your sister tell you that I fucked her hard just the way she wanted. She begged me for my big dick to be put inside of her. At first she was tight and I did not think she would be able to handle such a big dick like mine with all the crying and screaming but when she finally passed out I was able to fuck the shit out of her. I bust both her ass and p-ssy wide open. Then your bitch of a sister Rosetta waited until that next day to say I raped her, knowing she was a slut from the start just like you were when you gave me head." But when I saw Rodney getting mad and placing his hand back on the trigger I continue to taunt him by unzipping my pants and saying to him, "You sure know how to give the best head so for old time sake why don't you give me a going away gift, get on your knees like you did in the bathroom and suck my dick. You know you want to suck it; here I will even take it out for you, what's the matter you like it that night at Red Lobster." Rodney face turn hard like a rock, anger and rage escape his lips when he said, "Go to hell." Then officers came running out of everywhere yelling for Rodney to put the gun down, people were running, trying to take cover not to get hurt. I saw the bullet leave the gun as I fell down, not sure where I was hit at first until, I heard the officer yelling for Rodney to drop the gun and lay down on the ground with his hands behind his back. Five officers piled on top of Rodney yelling for him to stay down on the floor as they handcuff his hands behind his back, face down on the floor while another officer removed the gun from out of Rodney possession. But when they noticed the blank stare on the officer face, which was holding the gun, forcing another officer to walk over to him and further examine the gun then yelled out to the other officers that Rodney's gun was clear and it has not been fired. Whispering throughout the crowd broke the silence as they look on in shock and disbelief that the bullet was not fired from the gun. But once it was confirmed by the third officer that Rodney gun was still cold and there never was a bullet inside of the gun chamber. Which point to the fact that there was another gunman somewhere hiding out among the crowd of people? The officers spread out around the area searching for any form or type of clue that will help them capture the gunmen. Then they question every person that was in the crowd trying everything they could do to find the actual person that was involved in the shooting. I was lying on the ground with blood oozing out of my head. It didn't register in my head that I was shot until I heard the officer yelled for the paramedics because they had a prisoner with a gunshot wound to the head, that's when I knew they were talking about me. A groan escapes my mouth and for the first time I was able to exhale as I lie in a puddle of blood feeling no pain at all. In fact I felt free, no longer angry or any hatred in my heart but true desperation to live. My whole life passing before my eyes, all the females that I transmitted the virus to, and every black rose I passed out leaving my signature. I saw for the first time how much damage I brought these females and became the son of the devil. I felt the gate of hell opening up to swallow me up. The bright light of heaven appeal out of nowhere, open up and I could see this shadow headed towards me. I knew that I was dying and Rose was coming to greet me, then all of a sudden I felt the floor under me get hot then it open up, my skin burning and the smell of my flesh on fire. Could it be that the hell I made for Rose and all the other females; was the hell I come to make for myself? I had no one to blame for me being in hell but myself, everything at that moment flash before me. Thirteen beautiful females gather around me, each female placed their black roses on the ground around me as they walk by. The pedals from all thirteen roses on the ground formed the shape of my beloved Rose. As I took my last breath, I could hear the elevator door opening and I heard Brenda voice as she enter into the elevator, "Hi, my name is Brenda today is my birthday would you like to go out to dinner with me." I laugh then said my legacy lives on . . . .

About The Authors

KEISHA SEALS born March 10, in New York City, New York; she received a MBA from the University of Hartford. She attended SUNY Cortland and SUNY Old Westbury. Served in the United States NAVY; she was employed by the Department of Veterans affairs Medical Center as a Release of Information Clerk, Medical Record Clerk and a Program Support Assistant. She also worked for the United States Postal Service. Married to George Jackson Sr.; five wonderful children: Daquan Doyle, Shawn Seals II, Desaree Seals, George Jackson Jr. and LaTeashea Jackson-Mc Nair. Mother Helen Jones, two sisters Genelle Jones and Gail Jones, two brothers Jimmy Smith and Ali Doyle. Black Rose, The Final Thirteenth was her first book written in collaboration with LaKeisha Doyle and Desaree Seals. She has written a Poem book in collaboration with LaKeisha Doyle. She has several projects in the workings, a Spiritual book, Horror book and a Children's book in collaboration with all of her children, and many more to come.

LAKEISHA DOYLE, born March 12 in New York City, New York; she was named after her aunt. She has two brother and two sisters. She has a Poem Book out entitle, "The way I see the World through my Eyes"

DESAREE SEALS, born August 8, in Syracuse, New York; daughter of Keisha Seals. She is honor roll student with an A average and a member of National Junior Honor Society. She enjoyed collaborating with her Mom and Cousin on this book.